KARL WITH A K

Karl Lawrence

Pen & Pad Publishing LLC

Karl With A K
Copyright © 2014 by Karl Lawrence

Cover design by Karl Lawrence.
Author photograph by Michael Griffin.

Printed in the United States of America

ISBN 978-0-9833134-7-2

Pen & Pad Publishing LLC   jasmin@penpadpublishing.com
PO Box 34233   ⬜ /PenPadPublishingLLC
Washington, DC 20043   🐦/penpadpublish
http://www.penpadpublishing.com

Publisher's Cataloging-in-Publication Data

Lawrence, Karl.
  Karl with a K / Karl Lawrence.
    pages cm
    ISBN: 978-0-9833134-7-2 (pbk.)
    1. African Americans—Poetry. 2. Bronx (New York, N.Y.) —Social conditions. 3. City and town life—Poetry. 4. Youths' writings, American. I. Title.
PS3612.A9475 K37 2014
811—dc23

                                              2014905342

Other Books From
Pen & Pad Publishing LLC

Barrel Child by Pamela K. Marshall

Breaking The Cycle: A Barrel Child Story
by Pamela K. Marshall

The Men I Let Define Love by Janelle Williams

Children Are Like Cupcakes by Ansaba Gavor

Dedication

To Ms. Barbara Francis Spencer
"The stone that the builders rejected has now become
the head cornerstone."
– Psalm 118:22

PROLOGUE

Some people are born with a silver spoon in their mouth.
They have ways and means,
Never will they go to bed hungry,
Never will they go to bed crying from hunger pangs.
They have daddy and mommy,
Nanny and granny, auntie and uncle.
Their lives, from the start,
Are like fantastic adventures on magic carpets through a world without
difficulty,
Without suffering and without hardship.
They don't have a care in the world,
For they walk easily up a crystal stair straight to the top.
Others, however,
On the other side of life,
Are born at the very bottom of the socio-economic ladder,
To an unfair existence where there is no crystal stair to walk upon,
Just a dirt road or concrete pavement.
Night for them does not end when the day begins.
They are penniless,
Without money,
Without legacy,
Without family,
Without comfort,
And without a magic carpet.
Only by sheer willpower, may they pull themselves up out of the mud
And find their way in the world all alone,
And on their own two feet with their own two hands,
Sometimes on knees.
I am one boy such as these.
A child,
Born to the black, brown, and gray hues of poverty and squalor.
Born into a war-torn world,
Torn apart by vice and in the vice grip of evil and wicked persons,
In a neglected and forgotten corner of an inner-city slum.
I have, since the day I was born premature, lived in an unhappy home,
Many times neglected and forgotten about
By my forbearers;
Rejected
Also

By school,
Disaffected by the church,
And with no interest in the cheap thrills of the street,
It would seem that the world outside had turned me away.
So, I was forced then to turn to God,
And in turn, God turned me on to writing poems.
Without any formal education on the art form, and benefited only by
His Providence, I have adopted this craft as my own.
It is my life, my heart, my greatest love, and for the love of it I have
endured
The crushing weight of heavy burdens,
That would mostly cripple a person of less strength and little faith.
Under constant threat of eviction
And
Dismissal from school,
I have ventured outside of the box
Of my box-sized apartment, and
Traveled through the fire and through the rain,
Toiling for countless days and late nights
To write these poems,
And it is from those soulful depths that I have literally bled, sweat, and
cried them onto paper,
To serve as a raw and pure reflection of the indomitable spirit that abides
in me —
The same as the spirit that lives in you,
And to remind my fellow mankind of the many things
They've been made to forget in this day and age,
In the common language of common people.
Amen.
K

Starry Night

I have prayed all of my life
For a starry night.
And now the day has finally arrived.
My prayers have been answered.
The time has finally come,
For me
To carve out my place among the stars in the sky,
And shine my light
On the world.

Intro

"When righteousness is lost
And wickedness prevails
I appear on earth in bodily form"
(Bhagavad Gita: 4:7)

And now introducing...
Good evening,
Ladies and gentleman,
Friends,
Romans,
Countrymen,
Americans,
Negros,
Broads,
Whiteys,
Wops,
Crackers,
Spics,
Beaners,
Guineas,
Chinks,
And wetbacks.
Put your backs up against the wall!
Get back, sit down and brace yourselves for the ride.
Ready or not, here I come!
It's show time!
Allow me to introduce myself.
I be the dopest in the world, Special Agent K,
Also known as your daddy, baby,
Your teenage daughter's dream.
Congress' worst nightmare on Elm Street,
Quite frightening like a strike of lightning.
If George Clinton and George Carlin had a baby he'd be me, the baby boy Karl,
The love child of flower children and man-child in the promised land.
Trippy like a '60s hippie on acid and LSD.
Brothers say I'm tripping,
I'm hip.
I never slip when I leap over New York City skyscrapers in a single bound.

4

I can out sprint a cheetah and run faster than a speeding bullet.
Out Superman Clark Kent.
Out Jesse James.
Out Billy the Kid.
Hola! Senoritas come on down and squarrrrrrre dance with the most
dangerous angel of death, Dirty like Red Foxx,
Funkier than Parliament Funkadelic,
And obscene like a scene out of a hardcore porno flick.
I can out Lenny, Lenny Bruce,
Out Bruce, Bruce Lee,
Out Lee, Lee Morgan,
Out Morgan, Morgan Freeman,
Out Slick Rick, Freeway Ricky Ross and Rick James,
And shoot flames out of my tail like the Ghost Rider, Johnny Blaze,
Out Spiderman and his amazing friends.
Got more style than the Stylistics,
Bad to the bone.
I can out Scarface Al Capone,
Out sly Sly and the Family Stone,
Out gun Machine Gun Kelly,
Out Darth Vader
Out holy the Holy Vedas
Out bumble, a bumble bee.
The bee's knees to honeybee broads,
Pure like the sugar from cane juice, more juice than a juicer,
Looser than a sheet of loose leaf blowin' in the wind like Bob Dylan.
Outshine the sun,
Out water wet,
Out maneuver a super computer,
I hang out on Jupiter and Mars,
Inside of stars out of your grasp,
Trying to understand it is like grasping at straws out of your reach,
In the outreaches of space, spaced out like Space Jam,
Out of my mind.
Reproducing like a sperm whale.
Super K got spectacular semen to make a broad squirm.
I can out wiggle a worm.
Out Ravi Shankar on his sitar,
And
Out Jimi Hendrix on his guitar.
I'm an outcast,
That can outlast an everlasting Duracell.

Assault and battery
I'm a phenomenal anomaly, an outlier,
Wilder than a Rottweiler dog.
Karl can out killer a cop.
Out cop a killer,
Kill a racist cop for fun.
George Zimmerman, watch out!
I'm criminal and corrupt like a government official,
Official like Spalding basketballs, Nike and Adidas.
I can out run Run DMC.
Taking dimes out to lunch like Eric Dolphy and not spending a nickel.
I can out pickle a plum.
I'm 6 feet tall, dark and handsome
And in my spare time I enjoy going out for long walks on the beach.
My hobbies include ambushing Bushes,
Shooting at Rothschilds,
Throwing rocks at Rockefellers,
When I'm not writing, I spend my time traveling in my custom-made time machine,
Sneak-vicking vandals in the Victorian era,
Pissing people off,
Pissing out the window of my DeLorean at passersby on the overpass.
OUTRAGEOUS!
I can out caterpillar a butterfly.
I'm a super fly, fly wise guy.
Graduate from Cooley High School,
The heavyweight champion of cool.
Henceforth all eyes are on me,
The black man of the hour with
Soul power!
People! People!
Yes you can do everything you say you can,
Because I sure know I can.

ANIMAL PLANET

It was murder!
Happened faster than a sprinting cheetah,
And went by
In a flash of lightning,
Quickly.
Like the strike of a venomous cobra,
Thunder clapped.
The neighborhood wolf pack was out on the hunt,
When they ambushed the young pup.
What a shame!
He never stood a chance.
The look on his face was that of a deer in headlights.
The wolves fled the scene and disappeared off into the night,
Cackling like hyenas.
His dead body was now food for vultures and maggots,
Another mother bear had lost her cub.
She fell on him hysterical,
Weeping and wailing in her nightgown.
The sirens came,
And the pigs swarmed to the scene of the crime like locusts,
And
All the animals in town gathered 'round,
Then came the white sheet.
The cement was scarlet.
Damn!
His life was over...
Over what?
Now silver-back gorillas are out looking for payback on the monkeys
that did it,
And wise old owls watch in disgust from the street tops.
Another butterfly
Devoured by the spider's web in the game of wasps.
It's like a jungle, sometimes it makes me wonder,
Why?
Like animals, we feast on each other.

AUTOBIOGRAPHY

My name is Karl Omar Lawrence.
On the 23rd of June 1995,
I was born
Premature,
Four months early,
Weighing only two pounds.
I was small and tiny then,
But now,
I am tall,
My shoulders are broad,
My back is strong,
And
I am fit enough to run down a horse.
I am 16 and poor, more so than I have ever been in my life.
My feet are firmly entrenched in the dirt and grime of poverty,
Yet,
I am a poet,
Writing this to you,
Documenting my journey through
Life as I experience it.
And as I reach for the unreachable,
Understand,
That I am
16 and poor,
More so than I have ever been in my life.
Under pressure
And
Under scrutiny,
Because
I am underage,
Seldom understood,
Underestimated,
The underdog.
Undernourished,
Because
My mother is underpaid,
But still,
All through the day
I dream,

And
Think of the unthinkable,
Express the inexpressible,
The ineffable,
Move the immovable,
With human hands, reach for the unreachable,
With arms too short, change the immutable.
Time travel and fly through space,
Against all odds, defying the odds,
Swimming upstream against the swift currents of the mainstream.
A caged bird singing,
ME.
Making possible the impossible,
Doing the undoable,
Naming the unnamable,
There is no limit to the things that I can do.
I am without limits.
Uninhibited and unlimited.
Although,
I was born a mere two pounds,
I have now grown into a giant.
When I walk, my footprints indent the face of this vast earth,
All 196,939,900 square miles are mine.
For when I look up at night and see the boundless sky,
I envision myself among the stars, for I too am boundless and infinite,
And like a lotus flower, I have bloomed in the mud,
Far away from the light of the sun,
With one thousand petals more than I should have ever had,
When you thought it couldn't happen,
It did,
And it is,
And I am...
Karl with a K.
Nice to meet you.

TIME

Now that it's about that time, it's time to check time out,
But first, what is time?
Time, defined as the duration regarded as belonging to the present life,
As distinct from the life to come from eternity;
A limited period or interval.
Time!
Is slipping away from you this very instant,
And has been from the moment in time you were born.
Your time could expire at any given time,
Because time never yields, never forgives, never relents.
Time, co-existing with space,
Controlled by Father Time,
And
Father Time is no respecter of persons.
But let me explain it one more time.
Don't worry, I'll take my time.
This time, I'll take it slowly,
But time is of the essence, so make sure you are keeping track of time.
Whether Casio, Rolex, Timex, or Movado,
Analog or digital.
Whatever your preference,
Just keep watching your watch, and make sure to set the time to Eastern
Standard Time Zone.
What's your frame of time?
Do you know what time it is?
Because if not,
It's about time to get it together.
They say blacks are never on time for anything,
But it was a black man who invented the first working clock,
To tell time a long time ago in America, the greatest country of all times.
Home to
Muhammad Ali, the greatest boxer of all time,
And Michael Jordan, the greatest basketball player of all time.
Oh how time just flies by when from time to time, I reminisce on the
times I used to act up
And my mother would put me in
Time out,
But,
Times have changed.

Times are changing.
These are the end of times.
These are the times that try men's souls,
And in this time of crisis,
Time is critical.
Times are hard on the Boulevard.
Times are rough.
Growing up, I heard that time and time again, time after time.
I wonder if once upon a time, there was a time, when times were different.
You know, like
The good ole times.
The time of our lives.
Who knows, but Father Time?
But anyway, life goes on and time goes on.
The clock keeps ticking and as I become older and wiser, with time,
I sit back and take the time to watch the fools who take time for a joke,
The athletes, singers, actors and actresses
Who think that their time in the limelight
Will never fade out,
That they will never play out, that their time will never come,
And most ordinary people, spend their time here on earth wasting time,
Being wasted all the time,
Getting high all the time, screwing the time away, just to kill time,
Not knowing the time, fighting against time, running away from time,
And for the time being, you can run but you can't hide,
Because time is running out and soon your time will arrive,
In due time, time will catch up to you,
Because time waits for no man, and most don't realize it until times up,
When the time is too late.
Failing to capture their fleeting moments in time,
Until they end up
Frozen in time.

Synthesizer

Logging on…
Dear computer gods,
Synthesize me,
Virtualize me,
Microwave me,
Webify me,
Digitize me,
Into a bite-sized megabyte.
In a nanosecond make me live
Longer,
Younger,
Thinner,
Fitter,
Better,
Forever,
Computer-ful!
New and improved,
On the move,
On the go,
On the run,
On my iPod,
My iPad,
My iPhone.
Gratuitous consumerism,
Excessively accessible,
Instant quick-fixed,
Remote controlled silicon souls.
Mechanize my mouth and melt my mind-control into mush and microchips,
With digital crack crystals, Starbucks coffee and a large fries.
Supersize me.
Radiowave me.
Enslave me.
Stem cell my babies.
Magnetize me.
Hypnotize me.
Facebook,
Twitter,
Myspace,

Youtube and
BBM me.
Friend me.
Google me.
Gobbledegook nooks and e-Books,
Modernized, computerized,
Inflatable,
Portable,
Accessible,
Fashionable,
Wasteful,
Boastful,
Replaceable,
Disposable,
Restartable,
Electronic,
Robotic,
Supersonic,
Sodomy of the medulla oblongata.
LOL! Like my status.
My life,
My problems,
My responsibilities,
Brainwash my dirty laundry.
Rinse,
Recycle,
Repeat,
Repost,
Retweet,
Retarded,
Amen.

SPECIAL K, II

My fellow Americans, Friends, Romans, Countrymen,
Lend me your eardrums,
So I can continue to talk that
Jive talk!
The other night, I got into a fight with the Devil,
And whooped his behind.
Then threw Dante into the inferno with him.
I lassoed Leviathan, licked Lucifer and shot to Jupiter.
Strangled the serpent, and snuffed Judas for snitching,
And when Jesus was on the cross,
I pleaded with Pontius.
I was the electric light that knocked Paul off his horse,
And came to Constantine in his dream.
I remember one time Moses begged me to let his people go.
I was feeling generous so I parted the sea,
And let him and the Jews walk free.
Thou hath never seen another brother flamer than me.
Beam me up, Scotty!
Fly me up to space on the Mothership Connection.
Yes, yes, ya'll!
Check it.
I am the phantom that cracked the atom and dove 10,000 fathoms under
the sea.
I tipped the Berlin Wall over by accident,
Karate kicked Bruce Lee in the face on purpose,
Made Jack Dempsey roll over in the '20s.
I told you before, in the '30s, my style was dirty like the Dust Bowl.
Ask Dusty Springfield how I get down.
I get around and around like a merry-go-round,
Cooler than Bugs Bunny.
Casanova Iceberg Slim made Mona Lisa blush,
And turned Joan of Arc into a trick…
Just kidding!
I'm one of the livest that ever did it.
Write stone cold poems that'll turn Medusa to stone.
Super bad poems that petrify police and eat up Uncle Toms like Oreo
cookies.
The penmanship arsonist, I set fire to the Bronx in the '70s,
And rose from the ashes in 1995,

A Black Boy named Karl with a K.
16 years later,
I'm a rooting tooting, Wild-style, Wild West shooting, son of a gun,
Son of Sam, the son of man, in the form of a black man,
That can do anything a Spiderman or Superman can.

BLACK COOL

They call me Karl with a K,
There is nothing I can't do,
And nowhere I can't go,
Nowhere I haven't been.
I've been around the block.
I'm a voodoo chile,
A magic boy,
A black bohemian,
An outcast,
An iconoclast,
A child of paradise,
And chi-i-i-i-i-le,
Let me tell you...
I've done wrestled with an alligator, tussled with a whale,
Handcuffed lighting
And thrown thunder in jail.
I'm mean enough to make medicine sick.
Bad to the bone, bristle.
I rumbled in the jungle with Ali, and took the Champ in three,
The heavyweight champion of cool.
Froze for the picture for Gordon Parks,
And sat in the front of the bus with Rosa Parks.
My style was too sweet for Sugar Ray.
I turned blue-black Jack yellow,
Knocked him off his feet and made him see colors,
Then Hit the Road Jack
To run victory laps with Jesse Owens on the track.
I stole bases with Jackie Robinson.
I was Big Willie
Like Willie Mays,
Ain't no half stepping...
I'm straight with no chaser.
One time,
Round midnight,
I was feeling Kind of Blue,
So I got to drawing Sketches of Spain
For My Funny Valentine.
We made a love supreme and gave birth to the cool,
Real cool.

I blew my horn so bad, I made Dizzy Gillespie's head spin dizzy.
Cannonball heard,
And spread the word to the immortal Bird.
I hoboed and sang the blues with Hooker,
Came Up from Slavery with Booker,
And touched the Souls of Black Folk with Hughes and Dunbar.
I said I'm bad to the bone, bristle.
Funkadelic,
Sly and Stone cold.
Fam,
Been that way
Ever since I was a little black boy
Playing in Muddy Waters,
And a Gypsy Woman told my mother
I'd be the greatest man who ever lived.
Lo and behold,
I became a man
Spelled m-a-n,
Got the devil's charm.
Made
Devils tremble with Malcolm on the block,
80 blocks from Tiffany's.
I wrote poems that could kill with Amiri Baraka,
Took off my bible belt, and gave a whooping to every Klansmen
South of the Mason Dixon line during reconstruction.
The Holy Ghost caught hold of me,
And I told it on the mountain with James Baldwin,
Had a dream with King,
Doo'ed with the woppers,
Be'd with the boppers,
Hipped with the hip-hoppers,
And made it funky with James Brown.
I'm like a government experiment out of control,
Out of this world,
Out of my mind,
Ahead of my time,
And kinda ill with these poetic lines.
Listen,
I am one of the last poets,
The last of a dying breed.
I've been blacklisted,
Blackmailed and blackballed by the FBI.

COINTELPRO stuck to me like Velcro when I was a Black Panther.
Karl with a K,
The black Quetzalcoatl.
I've acted in plays with Canada Lee,
Harry Belafonte,
Sidney Poitier and Paul Robeson.
Caught a fire with Bob Marley
And wished upon a Black Star with Marcus Garvey.
Smooooooth.
Done laid everybody from Pam Grier
To Angela Davis,
To Jackie Onassis and Dorothy Dandridge.
Even had Nina Simone speaking in Spanish,
"No mas, no mas."
Sing it!
I lived the ghetto life with Rick James
And shot to fame with Tupac before he was shot,
I was Ready to Die with Biggie.
I'm Raw,
Criminal Minded,
Paid in Full,
Unforgettable like Nat King Cole.
Illmatic,
Straight with no chaser
And sharper than a razor,
A trail blazer,
From Samo to Pharaoh,
From Pharaoh to the world.
They call me
Karl with a K!

SOUL

Papa's got a brand new bag,
And at this time,
I'd like to give a salute to the wonderful, ninth wonder of the world,
Stevie Wonder.
Mahalia Jackson, who sang the gospel to the apostles of the Apollo.
The mind-blowing, Earl Father Hines.
The hollering Fats Wailer, and the sensational Temptations,
And I could never forget, the unforgettable Nat King Cole,
Or even Ornette, who shaped jazz for years to come.
I'm talking about that real, live, black music.
That jazz you hear, to move your rear, that R and B,
That rock 'n' roll, that funk, that soul, that swing,
That doo-wop, that Count Basie, lindy hop,
That Art Blakey, Nina Simone moan.
Young, gifted and black, on wax,
And them folks down at Chess Records,
Those Mississippi Delta blues boys.
I'm talking about the man, Bo Diddley spelled M-A-N,
Lightning Hopkins,
Robert Johnson,
Junior Wells,
Magic Sam,
Howlin' Wolf,
Leadbelly, B.B. and Albert King.
The real kings of rock n' roll, because Elvis Presley didn't impress me.
He wasn't man enough to shine Little Richard's Blue Suede Shoes,
But back to the topic.
Jackie Wilson could really rock it, and when Sam Cooke started cooking
at the Cotton Club,
The people started Stompin' at the Savoy, to the real McCoy Turner,
And I can't forget about the culprit who short circuited the Chitlin'
circuit.
With that I'd say, I'm talking about Baby Ray,
I met around Donny Hathaway, on Billie Holiday,
And I listened with Otis Redding sitting on the Dock of the Bay
Next to Curtis in a Mayfield of Minnie Ripperton's flowers drinking
moonshine.
To the O'Jays putting it down,
With Monk, Max, Roach and Clifford Brown.

19

Gladys Knight and the Pips were a trip,
And I had to R.E.S.P.E.C.T. Lady Soul, Aretha.
When I tried to rap to her,
Oh, Mercy, Mercy Me!
Marvin Gaye sang to me,
"What's going on?" he asked.
Let's get it on, I said to Sarah Vaughan,
Who really turned me on,
And oh, Ella gave me Fitz.
We did the Duke.
Etta James was so beautiful, when I saw her all I could do was cry.
I started jitterbugging, jumping with the joy of Jelly Roll Morton,
And got Dizzy Gillespie dizzy
To the beautiful songs of Charlie Parker and
Charles Mingus, ah um ah git in my soul.
I was mesmerized by the improvisation of Art Tatum.
Michael Jackson was a Thriller, and could play Isaac Hayes for days.
The Isley Brothers were some bad mothers... and I sho' nuff felt good.
Getting down, getting down to the funky sounds of James Brown.
Man that brother was super bad,
Like the super freak, bad boy, punk Rick James and Prince,
But when the Purple Rain clouds wouldn't go away,
Sonny Rollins came out, and the Saxophone Colossus beamed down on
us,
And then along came John Coltrannnnnne,
Who made a Love Supreme to Alice Coltrane,
And gave birth to Pharaoh Saunders'
Afro kind of blues,
Miles Davis, the king of Kool and the Gang, when Funkadelic took over
Parliament
With Earth, Wind and Fire.
I kept on getting down, getting down to Stax of Motown records.
Man!
Smokey Robinson was a smoking miracle.
That boy could sing.
Sly Stone did his thing, and was a bad to the bone,
Sex machine, like Al Green.
I'm talking about that black music,
That rhythm and blues,
That New Orleans swing, that rude boi roots reggae,
That rock 'n' roll.
Salute,

To the black musicians who played
With
Soul!

SOMETHING ELSE

Hot dang!
Oh lawd, Jesus!
Son of Joseph, and mother Mary,
Help carry me over the road.
Have mercy on my soul,
Cuz
These days,
Life ain't been nothing like a bowl of cherries.
In the rotten apple,
It's more like picking cotton, and being shackled in chains,
And I've been maintaining, writing all the day long,
But something wrong.
Sunni, what's wrong, son?
Sway
Yo'
Black.
Lately I haven't been able to catch the feeling,
And match the crack words together from scratch.
Like feather birds fly south for warm weather in the winter.
Seems like something's been missing.
What thing?
That Some
Thing
Like summertime,
Something
Exciting and striking,
Like lightning striking twice,
Frightening,
Enlightening,
Fingernail biting,
Fist fighting,
Attention grabbing,
Lip smacking,
Choke slamming,
Pimp slapping,
Chain snatching,
Chest thumping,
Adrenaline pumping,
Type of thing, to jump off the stage and kick off the party,

Make guns go off and set off riots,
Educate you and motivate you to burn a flag in the grass,
Piss out the window on the overpass and murder state troopers on the
turnpike.
That
Swerve on dirt bikes,
Dangerous,
Rebellious,
Something.
Go ahead,
Ring the alarm, punk, I did it,
And yeah, I said it.
You want it?
Come get it,
And we can get it on.
That word is bond.
Sing Sing,
Locked in the bing.
Revolution,
Something that
Swings like Tarzan with his private parts hanging out.
Outta sight, type of James Brown,
Get down.
Something
That bops like bebop.
Real hip,
And
Hop like hip-hop, and lindy hop,
That's improbable,
And
Probably
Unstoppable.
Monstrous like the Loch Ness Monster,
Colossal like a dinosaur fossil,
And indomitable like the abominable snowman,
And
Incredible,
Flavorful,
Something that's
Edible like chocolate
And
Unforgettable like Nat King Cole,

Coltrane soul.
Something different, something else,
Like the Boston Celtics when Russell was still playing.
Something that's smoooooth.
Something that don't follow the rules.
Something that's cool.
Something else
That's heartfelt,
Like a letter written with a felt tip pen dipped in blood.
Something with feeling,
Like the feeling of being in love,
To reel you in like salmon hooked on the fish line
Down in the bayou.
Brought to you by yours truly,
Special K,
The Secret Agent.
Over and Out.

Agent K

I-N-C-O-M-I-N-G transmission.
It's 007 from 782 Pelham Parkway,
Special Agent K, the Ace, reporting from base,
And I'm on a mission to seize and destroy the Who.
Who?
Yeah, Who, the culprit.
Who used the napalm in Vietnam and dropped the A-bomb?
Who, the destroyer of ancient civilizations, and the crippler of nations?
Who, the swine who ain't paid us reparations yet?
Who falsified the true story with his-story?
Who got the God complex?
Who, the forked tongued Devil, who gave life to Leviathan?
Who, the owner who got the country on lockdown with a master lock
and key?
Who, the conspiracy plot?
Who, the Big Brother?
Who, the all-eye seeing one-eyed Cyclops?
Who, the sly Fox News that got you trapped inside of the idiot box?
Who, the elephant and the jackass you vote for?
Whom do you trust?
Who, the FBI?
Who, the IMF?
Who, the CIA?
Who, the FEDS?
Who, the alphabet cops?
Who, the CFR?
Who, the Skull and Bones?
Who, the Bilderberg-ers, the real murderers?
Who, the real gangsters corporate thuggin' it?
Who sit at the Round Table?
Who, the world government?
The globe controller?
The stake holder?
The slave owner?
Who, the evil genius that hatched the AIDS virus from scratch,
And made it easy for blacks to catch?
Who, Monsanto?
Who, GMO?
Who, the unscrupulous pharmaceuticals?
Who manufactures the guns and gives it to the gangs?

Who makes the money? The laws?
Who sends your son off to war with a shotti to shoot at Saudis and come
back a mangled body?
Closed casket.
Who, the secret supplier of that junk that supes you up?
Who killed our prophets and profit from moving the product?
Who, the bloodline?
Who, the Rothschilds?
Who sent Assata into exile… meanwhile Pac was shot on the strip?
Who, who can't find out who did it?
And who *REALLY* assassinated Kennedy?
Who, the crook who COINTELPRO our heroes?
Who ordered the hit on Patrice Lumumba,
Kwame Nkrumah,
Jomo Kenyatta,
Che Guevara,
Huey P.
Malcolm and Martin,
And had Marcus Garvey marked for death?
Who spiked Bob Marley's shoe and drowned Jimi?
Who? Jim Crow?
Who supports the Klan?
Who's hiding under those bed sheets?
Who, the counter-revolutionary culture stealer war profiteer-er?
Who faked the funk?
Who stole the soul?
Our jazz, rock 'n' roll,
The oil, the gold?
Who runs all this, and makes the globe spin off its axis?
Who kicks back and laughs, while we fall off the edge of the map?
Who, the monopoly man?
The phantom menace we never see?
Who, the common enemy of you and I, the common folk?
Listen, whoever he is,
He better watch out,
Because I'm coming for him in a flash faster than Flash Gordon;
With an army of angry men and women armed to the teeth behind me,
And this time,
You won't slither out alive.
Sincerely yours,
Your worst nightmare,
Agent K

MY POEMS

All of my poems would be *BS*.
Unless they said what I meant, and I meant it when I wrote them.
More truthful than eloquent words, live words of which course through
my blood of course,
And no, I am not a romantic sentimentalist.
My poems are nothing like a gentle breeze wafting softly through the air.
They are more like tornadoes.
I want my poems to be poems that get in your soul, and send a shock
through your system,
From the top of your nylon wig to the soles of your Air Jordan's,
Like a death row prisoner in the electric chair.
I want poems that'll make you mad enough to think.
Think! It ain't illegal yet.
Poems that raise questions like,
Why we bake the bread, but they make the dough?
Why?
And who is they?
Who's the reason the rent is too high, and the water ain't running, and
the lights are off?
The same reason I had to write this in the dark.
Yeah!
Poems that raise HELL!
Poems of impassioned anger,
Radical poems that'll reach a whole nation.
From the streets to the schools,
The churches and corner barbershops,
The projects and penthouses,
From your house to the White House.
Militant poems that make the FBI nervous.
Riotous mob poems that'll leave corrupt trigger happy cops shook.
Poems that shake down sellouts,
Pull stickups on frauds and make slick, greasy-haired, house Negro
leaders
Run back to their colonial masters, with their tails tucked in between
their legs.
Poems that take the weapons of gangbangers and drug dealers,
And leave them dead in alleyways with tongues pulled out.
Put it on 'em poems!
Put it on 'em poems!

27

Butane gas and match poems. Nitroglycerine-like, explosive airplane
poems
That drop like bombs, when my words collide with your eardrums.
Arsenic poems, like smoldering hot, brilliant, splintering fires that'll light
the fire under your behind,
Evaporate liquor stores across the nation's ghettos,
And burn the nigger/devil in your heart to the point of near death.
Dagger poems that will finish the job.
Assassin poems that shoot the gift and kill all that whack, pseudo, new-
age,
Garbage that passes for poetry nowadays.
Poems that strike like thunder and roar like the ocean.
Half Godzilla, half Black Guerilla, family poems of power.
Power to make the earth tremble,
Move mountains and most of all,
Move you.
Let my poems shine like white incandescent lights and enlighten minds.
Let my poems strip me naked and lay my soul bare.
Let my poems speak silently or LOUD to black people.
No,
All people.
From my heart to yours,
Because they can stop guns,
But they can't stop my poems.

HARD WORDS

Now
Everybody over there and everybody over there
And everybody right there
And everybody
Up here
Tell me
Where
Are all the
Niggers
In the audience tonight?
Have you seen any?
Hip dicks or hunky funkies
Any boogie woogies?
Sookie sookie now,
Any boogie woogies
Here tonight?
Yoo-hoo
Jigaboos and jungle bunnies,
Any of you out there
Raise your fists in the air
Black power
Black power
C'mon shake your tail feather, darkies
Don't be scared
Come on out of the dark
Cause I can't see you from where I'm standing
Do I hear a nigger?
Going once
Going twice
No takers?
Well then, seems there's not a nigger in sight but
Not a problem
Cause got to be at least one kike?
Am I right?
At least
One!
Penny pinching
Long nose
Goldberg

One!
Jesus killer in the house tonight?
....no
What about grease balls?
Any Salvatore
Spaghetti and meatball benders in attendance this evening?
SERIOUSLY?
Because I
Really
Wanna know just where are all the
Real
Pizza dough spinning
Garlic bread
Eaters and beaners
Where the fence jumpers hop off to?
Where they at?
Where they at?
Orale, ese!
Adonde fuiste?
If there are any wetbacks drying off in the back row tell me
Spot a pollack?
Ayudame man
Andele!
Andele!
And oh
How could I forget
Faggots?
No faggots
Surprising
No dykes either
Potato picking
Mics
Nope
No hillbilly bobs
No hicks
No spicks
No slanted-eyed chinks
No, none
Whatsoever
What's going on?
Did all the niggers and the bitches and the crackers and the wiggers and
the spics and the mics and chinks and the wops and the guineas

Just
Disappear?
Ohhhhhh,
Wait.
That's right.
I haven't seen any because
There are none.
Not here
Not there or there or
Anywhere
Because everywhere I see only
Human beings
Nothing more
But
Certainly
Nothing less.

MACHINE GUN

He's manufactured in America,
41 inches, 31 pounds and black all over, in your town.
Hi-powered, he got the stamina to go 40 rounds.
New edition,
Certified,
Standardized,
The great equalizer,
Authorized and licensed,
And his name is machine gun.
I know you must've seen him on the news, or read about him in the paper.
He's world-famous or infamous,
Loved in the West hated in the East,
Despised in Vietnam and Iraq,
Despicable in Japan and downright dirty in Africa and Afghanistan.
He never seemed to get along with colored people, but his bullets are color blind.
He sees only in infrared through a 20/20 scope lens.
He's got a military industrial complex,
Head always somewhere in a mushroom cloud.
He's hotheaded and full of lead,
Easy to offend,
Pretend justice,
Arrogant trigger tempered,
Quick to blow your body to bits and think nothing of it.
Emotionless,
Terrible,
Cry crocodile tears of teargas,
Hurry!
Close your eyes,
Cover your nose,
Watch out and get down.
GET DOWN!
When you hear the loud mouth of the long barrel,
His voice sounds like a bomber plane hovering over a mud hut in desert terrain,
Where it rains
Acid and showers dum dums.
He got a loose tongue, so when he opens his trap and lets loose,
He'll slaughter your guerilla militia troop.

Shots ring!
Blaaaaaow blaaaaaaow!
Birds flee the scene and villagers scatter in a matter of minutes.
Brain matter is splattered all over the dirt road,
Bodies look like they're dropping out of the sky like flies.
Lifeless,
Heartless,
Little kids are running barefoot and naked through fire and smoke.
You hear their shrill cries and the screams of men, women, and children,
Brothers, sons, lovers, friends, daughters, and mothers.
To any other who dare to oppose you'll get mowed down, down to the
ground.
If you stand in the way, until no one is left standing.
Mayhem, massacre, macabre
Machine gun will pillage your village, brutally mutilate, maim and kill.
He loves to see bloodshed and spread the blood like mustard,
Torture body parts,
Heads detached from necks twisted out of place.
Dislocated arms attached to heads linked to limbs,
Linked to legs, broken bones and disfigured ligaments.
Eyes out of sockets,
Rocket launchers and flamethrowers,
Machine gun.
Gun 'em down!
Gun 'em down!
Dead like a dog.
Dead,
Dead,
Shoot red,
Bloodshed,
More dead,
More dead,
Murder,
Murder,
Merciless.
Kill!
Kill!
Kill!
Indiscriminately, in the name of liberty,
Yeah, kill, yeah!
Death, yeah!
Machine Gun!

Evil, devil, destruction.
Ohhh, yeah!
Havoc, yeah!
Machine gun, gun 'em down!
And
Murder,
Murder,
Kill, kill, yeah!
Agent Orange Juice, freshly squeezed,
Vietnam napalm, nitroglycerine bombs.
Yeah!
Hiroshima and Nagasaki,
Murder, murder,
Kill, kill.
Machine Gun!
Little babies, yeah!
Pregnant women,
Elderly ladies,
Shell shock 'em, drop 'em dead, machine gun.
Gun 'em down!
Blow 'em apart!
And
Murder,
Murder,
Kill,
Kill,
Kill!
Lie, shoot, rob, steal.
U.S. Steel, Exxon Oil, G.M., Halliburton,
Yeah!
Murder,
Murder, murder, more millions, and make billions,
Yeah!
Kill,
Kill.
Kill, for oil fields and gold.
Total takeover.
World control, warfare,
What is it good for?
But,
Murder,
Murder,

Kill, kill.
Murder, murder, and more murder, for more money.
It's
Good for business.
Machine gun.
OPEN FIRE!

THE MESSAGE

A message from the masses of the lower class grassroots...
Bring It On!
We, the mob that form like locusts and swarm like killer bees,
And right about now,
We're spilling out onto the street.
Watch the suit and tie squares spill their espresso, mocha latte, frappucinos.
Turncoats turn and run.
Sell outs high tail it the hell out of town,
And boys in blue catch the blue balls.
To the riot cops,
Go ahead!
Unleash your dogs and spray us with your fire hoses.
We have suffered too much and for too long to be afraid of a little water.
Shoot at us,
But your bullets won't cause us no pain.
No pain.
No pain.
You couldn't stop us even with canisters of tear gas, because we are done
with the
Cry-
Ing.
And the
Weep-
Ing,
And
Wail-
Ing.
We're through with the
Sing-
Ing,
And
Pray-
Ing,
Wishing and hoping,
And we've had enough of waiting and demonstrating,
Sitting in,
And lying in,
Rally-
Ing,

Picketing, petitioning,
Marching.
So now
We
Riot-
Ing!
Moshing!
Yelling and screaming!
Burn-
Ing buildings,
Looting stores and smashing windows, because we're hungry people.
Poor and angry people, that
Don't
Give
A
...
Up against the wall, Uncle Sam. This is a stick up!
Lady Liberty, lift up your skirt.
Pony the jewels.
What's the hold up?
Give up the goods!
Ring the alarms!
Call the National Guard.
Send for the choppers and the helicopters.
See what good that'll do.
After all,
What's an armored tank against an army of furious civilians armed with
Swiss army knives,
Rusty shanks,
Pitchforks,
Baseball bats,
Chains,
Hammers,
Razors,
Stolen grenade rocket launchers, and illegal submachine guns, under the
command of
Commander in chief,
Agent K?
We demand respect,
And will accept no substitutes.
No suppositions,
No

Ifs,
Ands,
Or
Buts about it,
No beating around the bush,
No meetings,
No peace treaties,
No panels,
No discussions,
No hearings,
No criminal justice courts, no fake red tape.
This time,
There will be no pretend justice.
No talk of no democracy,
No more hypocrisy,
No compromising,
And no negotiations.
We want reparations.
We want retribution.
We want restitution.
We want change.
It's revolution time!
And we want answers to our
Questions,
Like...
Who's the evil man?
Who's the corrupt man?
Who has misrepresented and miseducated us?
Underpaid and underfunded us?
Exploited us?
Who's the swine who has swindled us and stole from us?
Lied to us with false promises and cheated us?
Who's the consulate who has insulted us?
Who?
Who?
Come out from where you're hiding.
Where you at?
Where the President?
What the cuff is going on?
Why the rent and gas so high?
Where the bread at?
We want food!

We want clothes!
Which way is the White House?
Because we comin' in a bum-rush to cross the suckers on Capitol Hill.
I-N-C-O-M-I-N-G...
Stampede!
Occupy
Your
Street!
Knock, Knock!
Open up the gates
Or
We're kicking the door down.

WATER

Is odorless and tasteless,
Formless and shapeless,
But at the same time, all shapes, because water can shape shift,
React and adapt to vibrations.
Water is colorless, but necessary to people of all colors and hues.
After all,
Water
Is 60% of the human body and covers 80% of the earth's surface.
In ponds and lakes, rivers, streams, oceans and seas.
Beaches and islands that could just as easily be destroyed,
By the water from hurricanes, tidal waves and tsunamis.
Water is sometimes colloquially referred to as H2O,
And is a polar compound composed of one hydrogen atom and two
oxygen atoms.
Water is liquid at room temperature, freezes at 32 degrees Celsius,
And in heat, becomes water vapor.
Water vapor collects in the sky to form clouds.
Clouds become filled with water and water may fall to the earth in the
form of snow,
Sometimes sleet or hail, but usually does so as rain,
And rainwater can jack up your new hairdo, rain on your parade,
Or just collect in puddles and such until it evaporates, and nature's
process starts all over again.
Water is the reason why the sky is blue, but why is water wet?
Nobody knows because,
Water is a mystery.
Relatively incompressible and incomprehensible,
But nevertheless fundamental, and absolutely essential to all life.
Which is why in Latin, water is referred to as the
Fons et origo, the source and origin,
And the Hindu's Bhagavad Gita states,
"We have all emerged from the primordial sea,"
And it's true.
Because, once you were a little baby in your mother's womb, filled with
water,
And then her water burst, and lo and behold, you were born covered in
water,
And probably baptized in water,
Because water is a universal symbol for spiritual purification,

Revitalization,
Renewal and rebirth,
You heard the song.
Wade in the water, children!
This is a man's world, but it wouldn't be anything without water!
Man made a boat for the water, like Noah made the Ark,
Because the Lord was gon' flood the earth with water in the book of
Genesis.
Genesis, meaning Beginning,
"Because he hath created every living thing from water," said the Koran,
And it was the water in the Nile, Tigris, Euphrates and Yellow rivers
That gave birth to the world's earliest civilizations.
And the civilization of Atlantis, which is rumored to be lost
Somewhere deep underwater.
Water,
The transporter of the dead, across the river Styx in ancient Greece,
Of trading goods in commercial ships, and of
Dead Africans in slave ships,
During the Middle Passage, across an Atlantic Ocean,
That is filled with saltwater,
But there is also the freshwater to be found in ponds,
Mineral water, tap water, dish water, bottled water,
Ionized and flavored, enriched water.
Water in aqueducts, under the bridge, over the damn and in the soil.
Which reminds me to remind you to water your seeds,
If you want them to grow into plants
And water your plants to grow a garden.
They say blood is thicker than water,
But blood is 83% water, so where is the logic in that?
Without water you'd be just like a fish out of water,
DEAD!
But your ears are full of water, and you don't want to listen,
But, what more can I say? You can lead a horse to the water,
But you can't make the jackass drink,
Or understand just how vital is water.
When its summertime, 4th of July hot and we fiend for it,
To quench our thirst.
We wash wounds with it.
Wash our hair, our clothes, and our butts with it.
While dead fish are washing up on the polluted shoreline,
We buy 16 ounces for a dollar twenty five.
We bathe in it.

Iron with it,
Steam with it,
Cook with it and clean with it,
Shower with it, and in five minutes use more of it
Than a poor Indian family will have for an entire day.
Yet we go to amusement parks and play in it,
While 1.5 billion people are in desperate need of water.
Corrupt industrial cats make millions selling it.
Meanwhile every year 4 million people die from diarrhea caused by lack of water,
And other water-related diseases,
98% of which occur far, far away in the third world netherworld.
Where women walk an average of 3.7 miles daily to collect water every day,
Seven days a week, over a period of 16 hours.
That's four more hours than the half a day you spend laying on your behind.
Add it up.
Do the math, the next time you're relaxing in your evening bubble bath,
Or you flush five liters of water down your toilet, or use it to wipe off your sneakers.
Just think about it.
You only have to go to your sink for it, while most
Live without it.
Water.

IF I RULED THE WORLD

You know,
If I ruled the world,
I'd flood the earth and start the whole thang over
With a new race of man, made in my image.
In my world,
Every day would be like the first day of spring,
And summers in the hood would be cool like water
Flowing from an open fire hydrant,
And there'd be no gangbanging,
No drivebys,
No shootouts on playgrounds,
At family picnics or barbeques,
No petty fights,
And meaningless arguments.
Because, if I ruled the world,
There'd be peace.
The Israelis would get out of Palestine,
And there'd be
A permanent ceasefire across the warring countries of Africa
And the Middle East.
You could feel safe walking through the park by yourself after dark,
And go to sleep without hearing sirens and gunshots…
Or were they firecrackers?
In my world,
You wouldn't have to worry, because
Every little thing would be alright,
If I ruled the world,
You'd turn on the evening news and hear about all the murders that didn't
happen,
All the crimes criminals didn't commit,
And all the missing children that were found,
And about how
High school graduation rates were rapidly increasing at an alarming clip
all across the country.
If I ruled the world,
Graffiti would be legal.
If I ruled the world,
A whole lotta this madness would stop.
For starters,

43

All soulless, popcorn, pop artists would be out of a job.
Jimi Hendrix would come back from the dead
And perform live smack dab in the middle of a non-gentrified black Harlem.
The media would report the truth, *occasionally*.
Hot97 would play solid gold oldies and jazz classics.
Basketball players would not be paid millions of dollars a year
To miss shots, lose games, and get injured,
And
Black girls would take out their weaves and their extensions and try wearing their real hair.
Wheelchair patients would suddenly be able to walk again,
And drug addicts would be given a second chance right after a swift kick in the behind.
If I ruled the world,
I'd erase racism,
Capitalism,
Classism,
Sexism,
Terrorism,
And every other kinda –ism.
God would have no skin pigmentation or chosen people.
If I ruled the world,
There'd be no need for
Foster homes,
Food pantries or soup kitchens,
No jails,
And
No prisons.
The inmate population of Rikers would be the teaching staff
Of a street university.
If I ruled the world,
I'd restore economic freedom to
Third world countries and
Blow up the World Bank and the IMF.
If I ruled the world,
I'd stick a gun to the Pope's head and make him strip on television.
If I ruled the world,
I'd behead the President on the guillotine for having misled the masses,
And
I'd forcibly coerce criminal banksters to walk the plank,
And be eaten by viscous sharks in the Atlantic.

The good times would roll, like heads rolling from the gallows down
Capital Hillside.
If I ruled the world,
One nation under Karl with a K,
The emperor,
The furor,
The general,
The sultan,
The sheikh,
The Dalai Lama,
The sergeant and
The captain,
The commissioner,
Prime Minister of European Parliament.
If I ruled the world,
I'd still talk jive.
If I ruled the world,
I'd rule with a gentle fist.
If I ruled the world,
My world
Would have a smile
On its face.

THE PROMISE

Back when first we met,
It was fun, wasn't it?
That one afternoon that we spent together.
At the time, I had hoped that it would never end, but
Hope was in vain, as the wind whisked you away,
Just as quickly as fate had delivered you into my life.
So then, at last, our brief moment together had come to an end
And we were forced to part and go our separate ways.
Leaving behind only the promise that as long as the earth spun and
blood was blue in my veins,
That my heart would not rest, and my soul would know no peace,
Until you once and for all rested in my arms.
And with that, you were gone into the darkness of the subway staircase
And swallowed by the noise of the oncoming 6 train.
Bon voyage,
Mon amour!
You took a piece of me with you somewhere 1,000 miles away in France,
But even now that you are in what seems like the other side of the world,
On a distant and far off continent,
It is that promise that makes me feel as though
You are still right here beside me,
Watching the fountain in Washington Square
From the February cold of a park bench.
Do you remember?
Because, it is a memory that I could never forget,
A treasure that I cherish just like it was a precious jewel.
Now look what you've done, you really got a hold on me, Lucie.
Hook, line, and sinker.
Just like a fish out of water,
Don't you know?
I'd swim to the bottom of the ocean and pluck a flower,
From the sea floor just for you to wear in your golden brown hair.
You're the apple of my eye,
The beauty of the moon's reflection atop the waters of a crystal lake,
The radiance of the stars,
The grace of a pure white dove,
The autumn leaves in fall,
Chicken soup in the winter,
The scent of a rose on the first day of spring,

And the warmth of the sun on a summer's evening.
You are sugar,
Spice, and everything nice,
Cherry pie,
Cake and ice cream too.
That's why the thought of what you are could move a grown man to tears.
You make me weak.
You make me smile.
You make me sing.
Lucie, you are all things to me.
Among my heart's strongest desires and the fuel that ignites the fire of
my pen,
And trust that I will write
From
Night to day,
Dusk 'til dawn,
Day, night,
And dawn 'til dusk,
Until the promise be fulfilled.
Or else,
Birnam Wood would reach Dunsinane,
The sun would crash into the earth,
And life be no longer worth living,
And that's
A
Promise!

GUESS WHO

Guess who
Is the one who
Cried and prayed,
Night and day for me to
Make it out that incubator
Alive?
And,
Guess who
Breathed a deep sigh of relief when I finally opened my eyes?
Guess who
Carried me in her stomach
For five months, and went through labor pains when her water burst?
Guess who held my hand when I learned how to walk and took my first
steps?
Guess who stood by me when I learned how to stand?
Guess who talked to me when I first tried to speak?
Who was the first to hold me in her arms,
Hug me,
And tell me that she loved me?
Guess who was the last woman to mean it?
Guess who
Changed my dirty diapers when I crapped my Pampers?
Guess who,
To this day,
Washed my drawers and left them out to dry on the hanger?
Who? The same one who used to wipe the cold out of my eye,
Clean the boogers out of my nostrils, back
When I was a little snot nosed.
Guess who brushed my hair on Monday mornings
In front of the mirror before I went to school?
Guess who reminded me to brush my teeth?
Guess who gave me my name, this chain, and put the shine in my cross
piece?
Guess who bought me this $20 watch and taught me to wear it like it
cost a hundred?
Guess who dressed me like a million bucks, and tucked in my shirt, and
put the belt around my waist?
Guess who, with the same belt, beat the smart out of my smart behind,
When I got out of order,

And guess who could turn quarters, nickels and dimes into gourmet
dinners
When the rough got going,
And trust me, the going did get rough.
Guess who got up and went to work
Monday
Tuesday
Wednesday
Thursday
Friday
Saturday
And
Sunday
To keep her boy off the street, and the lights on?
And when the punk landlord turned the heat off,
Guess who pulled the covers over my skinny little chicken legs on frigid
winter nights?
Guess who
Fed me chicken soup when I caught the sniffles?
Guess who warned me the day before, to tie up my scarf and put on my
gloves?
And guess who
Found the missing buttons for my coat?
Guess who threw down in the kitchen every Thanksgiving and Christmas;
Who got that good corn muffin and turkey stuffing baking in the oven?
Guess who gave me my first bike,
Bandaged me up and dabbed peroxide on my cuts, when I fell off because
I rode too fast?
Guess who told me to slow down son, not so fast?
Next time,
Take your time;
In time,
Better times will come.
Just you study your lessons,
Read your Bible and
Don't you never *tun fool fe no gal.*
Guess who's my favorite girl;
Who I'd cry for,
Kill for and die for;
Who I live for and write for?
Guess who?
The woman that brought me into this world.

This one is for you.
From who else, but
Your
Only
Son.

PAIN

I was born without a silver spoon
On June 23rd Nineteen-ninety five.
Early that morning, the reaper came after my life, but he wasn't fast
enough to kill me.
So,
Ever since then I've been running.
My mother and father mixed my baby formula with Jamaican Rum and
Heineken,
And every day I went to school too broke to pay attention,
Buzzed by the contact from my daddy's marijuana habit.
He could never be there for me because, he was always somewhere high
atop a reefer cloud,
Rolling blunts, but wouldn't roll me to the zoo or to the park.
I suspect my mother partook in it too,
Too tired to raise me so,
As a child I introverted, drew pictures, and played tag with my shadow
all the time,
Shadowboxing with loneliness and losing.
How could I have known then that when I got grown,
Everything would get worse?
Now, I survive off of bread and butter for breakfast and crackers for
dinner.
Mosquitoes drink my blood in my sleep.
My apartment is overrun by rats running around and roaches,
Sometimes there is no electricity.
So I write in the dark.
No hot water to shower with,
No Christmas tree on Christmas, or a partridge and a pear tree.
Just a hand me down pair of pants and mismatched shirt to match.
I've been kicked out of school,
City marshaled out of my apartment, and tossed into the back of a cop
car.
Was it because I was poor?
Was it because I was black, that on my 16th birthday I wouldn't get a car
like the other kids,
And a job at my uncle's shop, that I had to wait in line at the Salvation
Army, as a knee-high,
And stand at the bus stop in the freezing rain?
Why so much pain?

My grandma would pray and rub me on the head, and tell me that you
don't deserve this,
That things will get better.
Yes they will, Grandma, by the willpower of my skills,
There won't be no more pain,
But for now,
I record it on paper and put it in my poems,
Because if it wasn't for poetry, I'd probably pack a pistol.

THE GHETTO

Otherwise known as the hood,
The slums,
Where the news cameras seldom come.
The barrio, the Boulevard, the projects.
Across the street
From the funeral parlor,
In front of the storefront church,
Behind the precinct,
Around the corner from the corner store bodega,
Next door to the liquor store,
Up the block from the drug spot,
The other side of town on the other side of Capitol Hill,
The wrong side of the tracks.
Nowhere in sight of the government,
Last on the president's list.
The Ghetto,
Where we're first in line on the 1st and the 15th,
And
First to be cutback, left out, and messed over.
Here, where the broken glass and garbage are everywhere and the air is
polluted.
Where it's Saturday Night Fever,
Sunday afternoon fervor, for the good news.
Monday's blues,
Tuesday's abuse,
Wednesday's he say, she say,
Thursday payday and
Friday night's
Flashing red lights, white lines and boys in blue.

GET OUT

Man,
This stuff is played out!
Day in,
Day out,
I get up and get out
Of my house,
And onto the bus.
The same overcrowded 12 bus that never has any seats.
That crawls underneath the tunnel and takes it's time inching its way
along Fordham Rd,
SIGH
Oh my god!
7:30 every day, the same time and in an hour's time, it will be time for
school.
Again, my gosh!
School, oh my! Oh my!
Day after day
I sit in class bored,
Counting the seconds,
Counting the sheep,
Day dreaming
Of being
Somewhere else please.
Anywhere but
Here.
2:30,
I fly through the doors back to the back of the bus.
Day after day,
The same tedium, monotony and mundane absurdity.
Day in and day out.
Everyday it's back to the same neighborhood,
That's exactly the same as I left it the day before,
The same.
Winos, beggars and panhandlers sit perched by the subway steps.
"Spare some change, please?"
On the crowded avenues FULL of EMPTY people,
Of boisterous teenagers and so called lovers holding hands.
Of McDonald's and fast food joints,
Of the neighborhood police on patrol,

Watching the same seven neighborhood no-goods,
Watching the neighborhood hoes strut by in tight pants that don't fit.
Day after day,
I walk past the same matchbox tenement buildings.
Back to 782, my building.
No key.
BUZZ
"Pizza delivery."
Works every time.
Everyday up the stairs past the apartments of
Wife beaters,
Chain smokers,
Drug dealers,
Single mothers,
And old skeezers
Passed their prime,
Who've been living in the same building
All of their wretched lives.
I don't want to be like them.
Dear God,
Please don't let me end up like them.
Back to the cramped claustrophobia of my apartment.
Narrow walkways and hallways lined with old pictures on dirt stained
walls.
There's no food in the fridge,
Rats dance on the stove.
My mother is not home;
If home,
Asleep.
And my father is at work,
But when she awakes, and he returns with a six pack of Guinness,
They'll go at it again.
First at each other,
Then at me, with that same old stuff.
You lazy bum.
You don't do anything in this house.
You don't wash plates.
You don't take down the garbage.
You don't work.
You don't pay rent.
You good for nothing son of a
Something something something,

Blah blah blah...
Yakkity yakkity yak...
Headphones in,
K out the door or off to my room.
They want me out one day soon.
Believe me, that day can't come soon enough,
But each day,
My room walls inch closer and closer,
And I'm
Closer and closer to the ledge,
And my feet hang off the edge of my bed.
I'm fed up,
I'm getting too big.
Getting to be a bother to my mother and father.
Too big headed,
Getting sick of this nonsense.
Day in, day out,
Living without
Anywhere to go,
Anyone to see,
Anything to do,
This place is not for me.
I gotta get myself together,
Get up!
Get out!
And get something.
It's now or never,
Do or die,
Because I can't just stay here
Letting the days of my life pass me by.
Day after day,
Day in
And
Day out,
I know
I gotta get out
The ghetto.

GUST OF WIND

It is not my wish to save the whole of the earth and all of its inhabitants.
For I am not Superman,
And I know that it is not in my power to hold up the sun, make the globe
spin.
And the oceans roar or color the grass greener.
Much less am I even able to number the stars.
What then could I do about the evil ways of men and women?
And of the world's ills?
I do not expect much,
But it is not my desire to fashion the world into a utopia,
For there were men who came before me greater than I,
Who could not achieve that end.
No,
It is not my wish to do the things that I know to be
Impossible,
Because that is too much for anyone to wish for.
Instead,
My only wish is that in my brief moment of time alive,
Here on earth,
That for as long as I am breathing,
To be like a swift gust of wind
That tips the balance of things,
However slightly it may be,
In what I believe is the right direction.
As for the rest,
Only time will tell,
And only God knows,
But since God, I am not,
I need not know what the future holds.
After all,
I am only a passing gust of wind,
And the future is out of my control.

GRACE

The sun, moon and stars,
The tallest oak tree.
The highest mountain peak,
The smallest grain of sand,
The tiniest pebble,
The calcium in your bones,
The red blood that flows through your capillaries and veins.
The breath in your lungs,
The food that you eat,
The mouth that you talk with,
The water that you drink to quench your thirst,
The feet that you walk with on
The ground that you walk on,
Your eyes,
Your ears,
Your nose,
And
Your very life
Is made possible only by God.
For everything that is,
All that you see here, can exist solely through His grace.
From the outer reaches of space to the dining room table,
He is every nook and cranny in every kitchen cupboard and cabinet.
Every square inch of these nine million square miles,
Every forest,
Every river,
Every ocean,
Every waterfall,
Every desert,
Every island,
Every block
In every city and town,
In every state of every country across all nations,
He is
The effulgent splendor of radiant Creation.
The warmth of a ray of light,
The cool of a gentle summer breeze,
He is the rain showers of April,
And the flowers of May.

He makes it snow,
Lightning and thunder,
And
It was He who made both
You and I;
Along with
Every little boy and girl,
No matter how big or how small,
Skinny or fat,
Short or tall.
He is the source of every plant, every animal, and the origin of us all.
HE
IS
The reason that we are here
On this planet.
The only One in our solar system hospitable to human life.
We are but temporary guests in His home,
Campers on His
Great green earth.
This vast expanse of endless beauty
Has been
Gifted to us
FOR FREE!
And all that He asks in return for His hospitality,
Is that we treat one another with decency and respect;
That every man,
Woman and child,
Every brother,
Sister, mother,
Father,
Cousin,
Daughter,
And son,
Honor the dignity of the other.
And...
That we give
Each other
LOVE!
It is a simple request, *really,*
For He has given us so much
And gotten
So little.

So,
Let us offer up our lives
As a
Humble
Sacrifice,
Because to do anything less
Would be nothing short of
Thievery.
Grace.

Words Of Wisdom III

And in the end,
As you stand at the crossroads of life and imminent death,
Your name and your fame,
Your family, your friends, and your fortune will be just as the dust is,
Gone with the wind,
And worth
Little more before the Divine Judge than the dirt in your grave.
Never mind what you saw or said.
Never mind what you heard about, talked about and/or joked about,
Because they are of no esteem in the estimation of God.
The only thing
That will matter
Is what you gave.
For it is giving that makes the gift that is this life worth living.
So listen,
While precious life is still yours, do all that you can to help your fellow
man and woman too,
But to the youth,
Don't be two-faced,
Tell the truth.
Treat your friend like a friend ought to be treated.
Respect your brother and your sister.
Honor thy mother and father, so that your earth days may be longer,
Because any day now could become the day where you no longer see
them;
Although,
You might not see that now, you must try to understand,
That you gotta work with your hands even if your fingers are bad.
People are often mean and inconsiderate,
But answer vinegar
With honey if you wish to
Extinguish fire,
Use water.
For love is the only remedy for a hateful and corrupt soul, and laughter
the best medicine.
After all,
You hear it all the time.
It is better to laugh than to cry, for when you cry,
You cry

Alone.
But when you laugh, the whole word laughs with you.
So, Laugh!
And be merry, but be mindful, and be kind, and be gentle.
Forgive and forget.
Let die,
And let go, for the longer you hold the coal, the worse it will char your hand.
Next time,
Keep it cool, with the fool.
Think less of his shortcomings and what he has failed to do,
And more of what must be done,
As long as it is worth doing.
Won't you please do it with all your heart?
Until you reach
Your heart's desire.
Follow your bliss,
But never follow the crowd, because the way of the world is wayward and wrong.
Instead, swim against the current to the other shore,
For this shore is no more than smoke and mirrors.
Be not deceived,
Tread the road less traveled.
Cast aside the lesser for the greater and greatness
Will
Be
Yours.
Simple!
So,
You needn't believe in magic,
You needn't believe in myth,
Or in hearsay and fairytales.
Just believe
In
Yourself,
And have faith in the power
That moves…

SALUTE

I-N-C-O-M-I-N-G transmission...
It's the Special Agent K,
Saying,
Greetings and salutations to all you very special people
That I have come to know.
This goes out to you, and you too;
Out to
Who else?
But,
Mrs. Genia Collins and all of yours, from yours truly,
And you know good and well that I truly mean it,
And to all my Beaner Mexican and Boricua friends,
Because whether
A wetback or jet black man,
A man is still a man, and
My brother is still my brother,
Regardless of his skin color or creed, and to
Mi carino, Norma,
Thank you for your warm hugs,
Kind words and observations
Oh,
And you know I had to show love to Mister Smooth Operator his'self.
Sunni Delight,
Thank you for shining on me, old man.
Salute!
To that cute copine of mine in France.
I'm coming soon,
So,
Stay tuned!
To Dawou,
I miss you.
Miss Paulson, and to mi amigo Christopher Rios, putting it down in the
studio.
To Akee, locked down in the bing upstate, and the gypsy from a place
in Oregon,
Home safe.
Salute!
To Jason Sway, my main man,
Stranded far away in the land of flip-flops, t-shirts and sandals.

At first, you couldn't handle it,
But now you got your act together, and I'm proud.
Salute, to the fair-weather friends that flocked around the females that
stopped talking to me,
And all the dropout salutatorians of the school of hard knocks,
That got the city marshal a knocking at their door.
Yeah, this poem is for
Ma chu'ch folk and po' people in the lower class section,
Section 8,
The whole 9 yards and the yard people, dem,
Salute,
21 guns!
For the crumb eaters, with roaches and rats in the front and back rooms
Of closet-sized apartments.
And to Lou, for teaching me hand skills.
To my teachers, I'd like to give a shout out.
To the foolish schoolboys that lacked the essential minerals and vitamins
to fight me,
Salute!
To my kinfolk and kindred spirits,
To Mildred and my future children,
The Bronx borough slum that I come from,
The block I live on,
The neighbors I live with and the thoroughbreds.
Born and raised like raisins.
That means,
K.T.
A.C.
C.C.
D
E
X
And everybody left with alphabet nicknames,
Salute!
To the nickel-and-dimers,
The old timers I spend most of my time with.
The nurses and underpaid nurse's aides,
And the rest of the mother loving nursing home I love.
To my mother and grandmother at home,
Salute!
To everyone I have named and the many nameless strangers,
Who number too many to remember at once.

And to anyone who ever bought me lunch.
To the buses and trains that brought me back to my crib,
When I had nothing but lint in my pocket and chewing gum in my gums,
Believe me, I really appreciate it,
Because no matter how high a bird flies,
It must come back down to the ground for food,
And I'd just like to say,
Thank you.
To those kind hands that fed me,
The people who didn't forget about me,
And the friends who kept me from going off the deep end,
Salute!

782 Kids

Photo by Kofi Sarpong

Acknowledgments

I'd like to give a special thanks to:
My mother and my grandmother
William D. Harper
Jason Swaby
Gina Collins
Norma Rodriguez
Marta Abigail
Mildred Speiser
Christopher Rios
Malcolm Willis
Lou Del Valle
David Irons
And the city of the Bronx, New York - my hometown

Contact me at:
karllawrence88@yahoo.com

http://www.facebook.com/SpecialAgentK88

About the Author

KARL O. LAWRENCE was born and raised in the Bronx, New York. He developed a passion for writing at an early age, delving into poetry when he was only 11 years old. His first spoken word performance would come just five years later at Riverside Park in Manhattan.

He was driven to write this book by the desperation he both witnessed and experienced in his young life. He intends to use his writing and performance skills as a tool to build a better life for himself and his family.

Karl is now a student at Howard University, where he majors in the art of being cool under pressure with a minor in making it look easy. When not wielding a pen, his hobbies include but are not limited to running, boxing, drawing and painting. He also enjoys politicking with made men and drinking tea in the company of exotic women.

Karl currently resides in Washington, D.C., and at this moment, he is in the kitchen cooking up more raw product.

Note From The Publisher

Dear Reader,

Thank you for buying Karl With A K by Karl Lawrence. I hope you enjoyed it.

As a small independent press, Pen & Pad Publishing does not have the luxury of a huge marketing department or the exposure of being on bookshelves across the country. If you enjoyed the book, please help spread the word and support this and future collections of poetry from Karl Lawrence by writing a review on Amazon or telling a few friends about the book.

Also, check out other Pen & Pad books by visiting our website:
http://www.penpadpublishing.com

While on the site, be sure to join the mailing list if you'd like to hear about new releases, book signings and events Pen & Pad authors will attend.

Thanks again,

Jasmin Hudson
Owner, Pen & Pad Publishing LLC

Pen & Pad Publishing LLC
PO Box 34233
Washington, DC 20043
http://www.penpadpublishing.com

jasmin@penpadpublishing.com
/PenPadPublishingLLC
/penpadpublish

CPSIA information can be obtained at www.ICGtesting.com
Printed in the USA
BVOW03s1314020514

352412BV00001B/6/P